THE BILLIONAIRE'S COMPULSION

THE BILLIONAIRE'S DOMINANCE SERIES (BOOK 1)

J. P. Valentine

Copyright © 2016

All rights reserved.

CONTENTS

1. Introduction
2. Chapter 1: Back To Reality
3. Chapter 2: Seductive Series
4. Chapter 3: Obedience To Authority
5. Chapter 4: Misconduct
6. Chapter 5: Thoughts Creep In
7. Chapter 6: Donovan's Compulsion

ACKNOWLEDGMENTS

INTRODUCTION

Donovan Hartwood stands, naked, in an empty and abandoned hallway. The lights around him are flickering, making it so his eyes have to slowly adjust to the strange darkness that encapsulates him. Unsure of exactly where he is, he looks confusedly to both his left and right, and sees a steel white door in the distance on his right-hand side. Walking up to the door slowly, he peers in through the single small glass window pane to find a disheveled hospital bed. Not only are the sheets carelessly discarded at the foot of the bed, but they're tattered. They're ripped as if there was a struggle. Looking closer, Donovan thinks he can make out black leather straps on either side of the bed, with holes large enough to trap a woman's arms. They're intimidating and thick, with small holes pierced periodically through the center of the strap so that they can be locked like a belt. Donovan feels excitement ripple through him upon noticing the straps. Straps like these are familiar, they're his friends, but for the life of him he can't remember being in this particular place before.

He goes to open the hospital room door, but it's locked. He jiggles it lightly at first, and then more aggressively, the large and unclothed muscles in his arms becoming taut and angry. Frustrated, Donovan Hartwood goes to look through the window. Maybe he can break the glass. As he considers punching the glass with his fist, it fogs. He can no longer see through it. Turning away from the window, he gazes down the dimly lit corridor and begins to walk, slowly at first until suddenly he realizes where he should be going. Picking up speed, he makes his first right and then keeps going straight, until he is confronted with what his mind and his body have both been craving all along.

At the end of the long hallway he can see a figure sitting in a chair. As he approaches the chair, he notices that the figure, upon seeing him, has started to squirm. It's a girl, well actually it's a woman, but her petite frame and slender face makes her appear young. She's wearing nothing but a white slip dress. Her pink nipples, erect because of his presence, poke through the slip as if they're begging to be touched. While her figure is slender, her breasts appear to be her most generous asset. Large and perky, her tits shift her entire dress with every squirm she makes. He would ask her a question, but she's been gagged. A black tie loosely covers her mouth and lips. *She's completely helpless*, Donovan thinks to himself as he gets closer and closer to her. The woman's arms are held down by the same leather straps that he had just seen in the hospital bedroom moments ago. Her ankles too are bound to the chair legs in which she's sitting by two more leather straps. She's been tied in a way that causes her knees to open, fully exposing the fact that she's not wearing any panties.

Who is this woman? Donovan briefly thinks to himself. He realizes that he's never met her. He chuckles to himself. He's been in countless positions like this before, but he's never really cared about who the bound woman was. For some reason, this particular woman seems different. He shakes off his hesitation, and with a smirk begins to advance towards her breasts. He's hungry to touch them, but at first merely stands over her as she looks at him. Her expression is of a pleading nature, but he's not sure exactly what she wants. After staring at her for what seems like eternity, he abruptly takes the nipple of one breast in his hand, and gently caresses it between his pointer and middle fingers. The woman shudders and gasps, wriggling as if she's experiencing both pain and pleasure. Enjoying watching her reaction, he takes the full breast in his hand and leans down to suck on it. Upon feeling his lips on her breast, the woman lets out a moan, fully indulging in the pleasure that he's giving her. Not wanting her to get too worked up, his lips release her nipple and he stands up straight. He begins to stare longingly into the void where he knows her panty-less lips await. He glances down at himself, noticing that his cock is fully erect and throbbing. His hand reaches to feel her wetness when suddenly...

She's standing before him. No leather cuffs, no more tie over her mouth. They're both standing face-to-face, naked but the dominance that he had over her is gone. Frustrated once more, he goes to grab her roughly, but finds that for some reason he can't touch her. It's as if she has an invisible force field around her perky and tight body. *Who is this woman?* Donovan thought to himself, with his arms outreached as he tried to grasp onto someone who couldn't be easily touched. *Who is this mystery woman?*

CHAPTER 1

BACK TO REALITY

Donovan Hartwood's alarm goes off promptly at 7:01 AM each morning. This extra minute of sleep allows him to feel more awake throughout the day. In fact, he demands that he's woken up promptly at this time each morning, and if he's disturbed a minute too early or a minute too late, his alarm clock will pay the price. Of course, Donovan never mentioned this to anyone, but another reason why he insists on being awoken at this exact time is because it's rather difficult to accomplish. You see, Mr. Hartwood's alarm clock is different from most people's. It's not made of plastic or metal. It's doesn't sing a repetitive song each morning until he groggily turns it off only to turn back over and snooze. No, Mr. Hartwood's alarm clock is a person.

And not just any person. Standing at five feet and seven inches tall, Nina is a blonde beauty whom Mr. Hartwood has the pleasure of being woken up by each morning. Donovan's wealth has afforded him the opportunity to require that all of his butlers, maids and other staff members wear uniforms as a job requirement. Hiring only women, his palatial estate is populated with maids wearing skirts that are two inches too short and butlers who must fill out the low-cut blouses with his emblem, DH on them. You'd think that there would have been a law suit by now about the inappropriate outfits that he forces his women to wear. But the truth is, they like it. They enjoy having their breasts stared at and being watched as they walk away from Donovan and his guests with their butt cheeks slightly exposed. With each employee receiving at least $100,000 per year to work for him, most of these women feel grateful for what Mr. Hartwood can offer, financially and otherwise.

On this particular morning, Nina walked silently to the side of Mr. Hartwood's bed and seductively whispered into his ear, "Mr. Hartwood, it's time to wake up." This is what she said to him each morning, after which she would help him to roll over and massage his back. In her former life, Nina was a renowned masseuse within the celebrity community. This is how Donovan Hartwood had initially met the woman. As Donovan rolled over, lazily preparing for the massage he was about to receive, he glanced at the clock. It read 7:10AM. As Nina had sat on the bed behind Donovan, preparing to massage his shoulders, he roughly pushed her off of the bed. Surprised, Nina gazed up at him from the floor. Not only did this permit Mr. Hartwood to see completely down her blouse, but it also allowed him to tower over her from his superior position.

"Get up." He barked the order at her. Timid and meek, Nina got up quickly, brushing down off her skirt and looked down, not wanting to meet his gaze. She was holding her hands together in front of her, as if praying that he will be kind and forgiving.

"What time do I wake up?" Donovan asked her, already knowing the answer.

"7:01", Nina replied sheepishly, almost in a whisper.

"And why did you wake me up late, Nina? What was so important to your busy schedule that you had to alter mine? Please, enlighten me."

Donovan was toying with her. While he wanted to see how she would respond, he already knew where this was headed.

"Well...you see, I had to change your laundry and then one of the other maids, Ingrid, she needed some help rearranging the..." Her voice trails off. Donovan's index finger presses against her lips.

"It's stated in your job description that you must wake me up at exactly 7:01AM. Maybe I should invest in an alarm clock and release you from your duties." Donovan says this with a sneer, knowing that Nina won't like these words. He's right.

"Please Mr. Hartwood, sir, please, I'm sorry. I'll be more diligent. I know how important your time is, sir." Now she's looking right at him, trying to convince him with pleading eyes not to fire her.

"If I don't fire you then you must be punished.

You seem like a smart girl but you make silly mistakes. Punishing you will remind you to be more aware of the time, and remind you that my time is much more important than yours. Come here. Lie down on the bed and wait for me." After administering these instructions, Donovan gently led Nina to the bed where he had her lie down with her legs dangling. The interaction between the blanket on the bed and Nina's skirt was causing it to rise, fully revealing the skimpy black lace thong that was also a required aspect of the dress code at the Hartwood estate. As Nina foolishly tried to pull her skirt down, Donovan took her hands and roughly placed them back onto the bed.

"You're not to move until I give the instruction." Donovan's words were icy. Nina, not wanting to anger him more, obediently kept still. Still standing over her while she lay helplessly on the bed, Donovan pulled up her skirt more and brusquely pulled on Nina's thong underwear. It snapped loudly against her soft skin, causing her to gasp in response. Then Donovan left the room, leaving Nina to herself. She felt as if he had been gone for an hour. Her bare bottom was becoming chilly and her she could feel her pussy tingling at the thought of what Donovan was going to do. While his anger frightened her, it also made her feel slightly weak in the knees.

When he returned, Nina laid in the same position. First checking to make sure that she hadn't moved, he then walked to the side of the bed so that she could see him. In his hand was a small black leather paddle. Finally, he spoke. "I have decided that your punishment will be twenty-five spankings for your tardiness this morning. Hopefully these lashings will teach you to be more prompt. If you cry out, the lashings will intensify. It's best if you keep quiet, so I can do what needs to be done in peace." With these words floating in the air, Donovan gently pulled down Nina's thong so that it hung loosely by her knees. He then took the leather paddle and took his time rubbing the long end of it in the spot where her thong previously was. Without warning, Donovan smacked Nina's bottom with the wide edge of the paddle, causing her to jump in surprise. He continued over and over again, increasing the intensity only slightly. His goal was to make her bum look red while keeping the pain she felt to a minimum. His primary goal was to arouse her, not abuse her. *Smack. Smack. Smack.* He enjoyed watching the weight of her juicy seat bounce up and down tightly each time the paddle made contact with her smooth and pale flesh.

Donovan's need to control the women whom he employed went beyond simply a boss-employee relationship. He wanted, in some ways *needed*, the women who worked for him to lust after his touch and his attention. In his heart of hearts, he has never been able to figure out exactly what the reason was why he pursued and seduced women in this way. His primary goal when he punished his women was never to hurt them. Instead, he sought to control them and arouse them through this control. He needed to feel like he was in charge. With each *Smack* that he heard through contact with Nina's soft and supple flesh, Donovan could feel his cock twitching with more and more tension rising in it.

Nina was quiet at first, listening to Donovan's instructions to not move and not make a sound. But as Mr. Hartwood kept administering the spanks, she could no longer contain her voice. Nina's moans were becoming increasingly audible. With each spank she sounded less like she was in pain and more like she was enjoying what was happening. What's more, by Donovan's tenth spank to her rump

Nina actually was pushing her pelvis up to meet his paddle, excitedly meeting the end of his punishment instrument. Donovan, as he stood there shirtless and strong, could see the way in which Nina was reacting to her punishment. Just as abruptly as he had started to implement her punishment, he stopped spanking her. Feeling strong and robust after causing this innocent and busty woman to become ripe with sexual energy, Donovan greedily dipped one of his fingers into Nina's wet and waiting vagina. Her dripping pussy proved to him that she had become heavily aroused after being spanked. He wiped his finger on her back, not wanting to contaminate his own fingers.

"This was supposed to be a punished, Nina. I am beginning to think that you enjoyed the spanking that you deserved."

"No, sir", Nina panted, trying to conceal her arousal and excitement. "I've learned my lesson. I will wake you up on time for as long as I continue to work here." As she spoke, he could see that she was sort of wagging her rump in the air, as if hoping that their interaction would continue. Donovan stared at her reddened ass briefly, suddenly becoming bored and indifferent. He didn't care what she wanted. She was only his maid, there to serve him as he please.

"Put your panties back on, my dear. I have to get on with my day." Donovan took he hand and cracked it against her bum for one last satisfying *smack* before turning his attention away from her and back onto his daily routine. *Besides,* Donovan briefly thought to himself, *I have to save myself for later.* He turned and began walking towards his luxurious private bathroom. Standing naked in his bathroom, he looked at himself admiringly in the mirror. His cock, having been aroused by the punishment he had just given his naughty employee, stood erect and at attention. An impressive ten inches long, his penis seemed to compliment his dominant and controlling personality. Standing tall and erect, it looked like it could administer much more pleasure than a simple leather paddle ever could. For a moment, Donovan took his cock in his hand and gently stroked it, knowing exactly how he planned to relieve himself of his aching erection. His strokes increased in intensity as he thought about his prize, waiting for him at the end of the day, or whenever saw fit. Picturing her, bound and eager to please him, he almost caused himself to prematurely release the pressure of his erection. Knowing that if he continued he would be sure to bust, Donovan stopped stroking his large cock and instead got into the shower.

CHAPTER 2

SEDUCTIVE FAMILY SECRETS

Before moving into the bathroom, Donovan paused at the large doors that opened up to the balcony jutting off of his second story bedroom. Upon looking out the window, Donovan's eyes were greeted by the sun's rays pouring over the peaks of the distant Diablo Range; illuminating the palette of greens, yellows, and browns in the lush valley below. It looked to be a beautiful day; made only more resplendent by the sprawling decadence of the Hartwood Estate. He looked down to the stables, where he caught a glimpse of the graying muzzle of Stag, the beautiful stallion that had been his since he was old enough to saddle, peeking out into the morning calm. Beyond the corral, the gentle waves of the lake twinkled like stardust as the masts of the 40-foot schooner, The Half-Mast, bobbed silently in the dock. He heard the trickling of the tall Venetian fountain that stood prominently in the middle of the sandstone-paved courtyard. A gentle wind caressed his cheek and he turned towards the burgundy arches that adorned the second floor of the west wing. A slight feeling of anxiety crept up his abdomen as he gazed out at the exterior wing of the house where his father, Walter Hartwood, lay motionless; as he would likely remain until the monitors that surrounded his bed would stop their incessant beeping.

Walter Hartwood was the paragon of the Silicon Valley success story. He made his immense wealth through the development of technology related to self-driving vehicles. His claim to fame was the development of the complicated algorithm that kept self-driving vehicles from running into other cars and trees while on the road. After selling this algorithm to Google, Walter was a self-made billionaire. He continued his career with Tesla, the first self-driving car company, and brought Donovan under his wing as soon as he was old enough to start working in the family business. Donovan proved to be a quick learner, and by the age of twenty-two his father and the other board members of his company, Hartwood Industries, Inc., had given Donovan a controlling partnership. Always proud of the family name, Donovan dedicated his life to advancing his father's work. His drive and fearless ambition helped him gain quite a reputation in the business world.

It was lucky that Donovan worked so hard, because at the tender age of twenty-five his father was hospitalized after suffering from a massive stroke. He became inert. Spending his days being cared for by a nurse in his own wing of the Hartwood estate, there was little more than a pulse to indicate that Walter was still alive. Donovan saw that he was given the best treatment possible, but there was little that could be done to reclaim the great vitality and fortitude the man used to carry. The stroke occurred three years ago, and Donovan, now twenty-eight, had taken on the responsibility of running his father's business, as well as inherited control of the company's funds. Donovan had become the face of Hartwood Industries practically overnight.

The Hartwood Estate can be best described as truly something out of a dream. Donovan had his own private helicopter, and the property even had its own indoor ski resort, which he would frequent with his snowboarding friends when the weather was cold and the need for exhilaration was high. Donovan spent his summer days sailing to obscure as well as fun parts of the world, like South America and Miami. Not much of a bookworm, Donovan had been homeschooled from a young age, with his education being primarily tailored to learning about how his father's business operated and how he could best help with business growth over time. This being the case, he was able to learn as he traveled the world. While he was able to develop himself culturally through these means, this type of upbringing also made Donovan feel extremely elite, as it would anyone. He had the world at his fingertips, literally, and with a monthly severance of one million dollars from his father, Donovan was able to do what he wanted, when he wanted. As would probably happen to anyone in his position, Donovan became more and more big-headed and arrogant the older he got. Luckily, it seems as though he handsomeness grew in time with his arrogance, so he was able to get away with being rude and demanding with little to no consequences.

While Donovan's upbringing was anything but traditional, his parents also treated him in rather unconventional ways. Donovan did not start the tradition of hiring only women to work at the estate. His father, Walter, was the true originator of this tradition and saw to it that only women worked on the property at all times, no exceptions. While it might seem obvious that Donovan's mother, Astrid, would have a problem with this, she was often too preoccupied with her own social gatherings and elite events to notice that her husband was a bit too friendly with some of his employees. Or at least that's what she would have her friends and other types of people believe. While Walter's infidelity generally went on for years inside of the Estate with little to no public mention or problem, there was finally one woman who sent Astrid over the edge with jealously and ager. This woman was Donovan's tutor and nanny, Gianna, and she finally sent Astrid into a much overdo frenzy.

What was most conflicting for Donovan was that he still remembers Gianna to this day. She was his first crush. He was positive back then, at the age of thirteen years old, that their twelve-year age difference would be no obstacle for their love. Gianna was not only beautiful, with her brown hair always cascading down her back in waves, but she had also been endowed with a perfect hourglass figure. As a blossoming teenager, it was hard for Donovan not to notice Gianna's curves as she tutored him on the ins and outs of his father's business; however, it soon became obvious to Donovan that his father also took an extra interest in everything that Gianna had to offer his son. Donovan would often see his father and Gianna taking walks together along the property grounds and took notice that their hugs goodbye would always linger. This behavior seemed erratic for his father. Typically, Walter would fancy one of his employees for only a week or two, becoming bored rather quickly. Gianna and he remained companions for years.

That was, until one day Astrid caught the two of them in a rather unspeakable act. Coming back early from her tennis practice one afternoon, Astrid had decided that she was going to head to the gym's sauna to relax and exfoliate her skin. Astrid too, was one delicious looking lady. Of Norwegian descent, Walter and her had become acquainted while he was on a ski trip through the Netherlands.

Over thirty-years younger than her at the time, Astrid used her high cheek bones and slender figure to persuade Walter into marrying her and bringing her back to America. Unfortunately, it wasn't until she was in the states that Astrid found out how demeaning and misogynistic Walter truly was. She was introduced to Walter's female-only staff, and was told that in order to be his wife, Astrid must agree to keep to herself most days. Instead of fighting him, Astrid initially agreed. She couldn't deny that the Hartwood Estate was grandiose. Her life had the potential to be lavish.

She tried her best to ignore her husband's infidelity, but after a particular incident at the gym's sauna, Astrid decided that she had had enough. Having just got done tennis practice, Astrid had her headphones in and was bopping along to the Rolling Stones (her favorite rock group) as she approached the doors to the sauna. As she walked into the darkness and settled onto the sauna's hard bench, she could see two figures in the far corner of the room. Taking a closer look, Astrid's mouth slowly gaped open as she saw Walter standing over a woman who was kneeling on the floor and whose hands were behind her back. Both naked, they looked at Astrid with surprise. As the shock on Astrid's face turned into pure rage, Walter turned towards her, giving her a full-frontal view of his hard and erect penis.

"Care to join us, love?" Walter said, with a sly smile on his face. He then turned back towards the kneeling woman, and Astrid got a good look at her. It was Gianna. Astrid could see moisture pooling on the upper curves of her breasts due to the the heat of the sauna room. She could see Gianna's nipples, pointy and erect from both the excitement of sex and the excitement of being caught. Gianna rose from her knees and walked towards Astrid.

"I'm sorry, Astrid. Please, come in, I can make all of this feel better for you." She tried to take Astrid's hand, but Astrid pulled away, not wanting to engage in such promiscuous behavior with her dishonest husband. Although she felt hurt, Astrid would have been lying if she were to say that the sight of Gianna wasn't slightly pleasing to her. Astrid could see plainly that Gianna took great care of her mound. Cleanly shaven and neat, her vaginal lips looked tight and seductive. For a brief moment, Astrid imagined if Walter were not there, how she would consider taking Gianna's hand and go with her into the abyss of the sauna mist. She imagined standing here, feeling Gianna's busty curves against her own, kissing the pooled moisture off of her big and perky breasts. Truth be told, Astrid felt herself becoming a bit envious of the fact that Gianna's large and perfect breasts managed to stand against the influence of gravity.

Instead of indulging in her brief and instinctual thoughts, Astrid turned from the sauna and quietly exited from the gym. She told everyone that she could at the Estate about the interaction that she had witnessed between her husband and Gianna, in hopes that this would get Gianna fired. She told so many people that even Donovan found out. He was heart-broken. While he had hoped that Gianna would be able to keep her job, he also hoped that it was all a lie, and that his father had not truly taken pleasure with his crush in this way. Instead of becoming angry, Donovan waited, hoping to hear that his father was sorry and that it wasn't going to happen again.

A few nights later, after a charity gala that Astrid and Walter had attended together, Walter confronted her about her loose mouth regarding the incident with Gianna. The liquor had been flowing at this particular party, and Walter had decided to take this opportunity to mince no words.

"You know; I'm not going to stop seeing Gianna. You saw her naked, you know how irresistible she is. If you have anything else to say about the matter, let's hear it now. Otherwise, I demand you stop spreading rumors about what happened. As the owner of this estate, I have a reputation to maintain." Walter waited, anticipating a fight, and that's exactly what he got.

"If you keep seeing Gianna, I'll start hiring men to walk around this place who will wear just as much as your women wear now. I'm sick of you looking at all of the women around here with such lust. We barely have sex anymore." Astrid spat the words at him, hoping to stir some sort of regret in him.

"Astrid, dear, you don't own this property. You have no right to start hiring men to keep the grounds. Plus, my current employees certainly perform adequate work as it is." Walter smiled and started to walk towards his wife, secretly knowing that the phrase "adequate work" held more than one meaning. He grabbed onto both of her arms, and looked into her eyes sternly. Astrid cowered slightly, and struggled to escape his grasp. Walter tightened his grip, refusing to her release her.

He continued, "Since you signed a pre-nuptial agreement, I do not want to divorce you. It's lucky for me that you're good looking, so I will agree to keep you around at the Hartwood Estate. You will be given a monthly allowance, and I will see to it that you are taken care of in every way. However, I do not want to interact with you. You will be condemned to live in the west wing of the estate, where the arcade and the movie theater are located. Additionally, you will still be required to engage with me sexually whenever I see fit. This will be your punishment for trying to force me to act in ways that are not natural to me. You see, Astrid, I am a billionaire. As a billionaire, I do as I please. At one point, I thought that I wanted to be married to someone and wanted to have a monogamous relationship with you. Now, my desires have changed. I no longer require your assistance as a wife, and I will keep you instead as a lover. And one last thing, your duty to me will include participating with any other woman that I bring into your side of the house. You see, sometimes I enjoy seeing women please one another. I have thought about you and Gianna licking each other in unmentionable places. And judging by the way I saw you looking at her the other day in the sauna, I am guessing that you too have thought about sucking and licking her most intimate areas. I have decided that you two will come to bed with me tomorrow evening. If you don't like this arrangement, you can think of it as another punishment for the fact that you disobeyed my wish and did not come into the sauna with Gianna and I the other day." Walter's eyes were searching in Astrid's for some sort of recognition or defiance. He slowly advanced his face towards hers, forcing her to kiss him. Feeling helpless, Astrid conceded. Having no options, family or friends in the United States, Astrid didn't know what to do. Finally, she spoke.

"Okay, Walter. I will do as you say." He finally released his grasp from her. She was free to go.

Over time, Gianna also became old news to Walter, but Donovan could never forget the way in which his father treated the women he encountered, especially his mother. After this incident, Donovan watched his mother become a miserable fixture at the Hartwood Estate. Never happy, Astrid would constantly berate Donovan about how lonely she was. Walter, on the other hand, would tell Donovan that his mother was the type of woman Donovan should never want to be with. "No woman should be demanding of you, Donovan. You should always call the shots" Walter would tell his son, encouraging him to pursue only the most voluptuous and sexy women he could find. "You have the money and the looks, Donovan. Women are often more attracted to money than they are your appearance anyway. Remember that." With these memories etched into his head, Donovan became more and more like his father. He saw women as objects that could please him. Nothing more, nothing less.

CHAPTER 3

OBEDIENCE TO AUTHORITY

As Donovan got out of the shower, it was obvious that he was no longer as turned on as he was when he was punishing Nina. His penis had become soft and less distracting; however, if a woman had been in the shower with him it would still be hard to ignore his chiseled abs and lean physique. The muscular cuts on either side of Donovan's pelvis looked like they were arrows inviting the eyes to gaze at his big and full package.

His face was similarly chiseled and tight, with a prominent Adam's apple protruding dominantly from his throat. As he stood on his bath mat drying off, even he had a hard time not looking in the mirror at himself. Having scheduled a meeting for 9:30, Donovan knew that he had to hurry if he wanted to make it to the office on time. In addition to the time, Donovan saw that he had received a text message while he had been lathering. He was pleasantly surprised to see that it was from his secretary, Charlene. The text read:

8:45AM: *Good Morning Mr. H, reminding you of your meeting at 9:30 with the shareholders. Please let me know if you need anything - C*

Donovan paused, reading the message with some amusement. *Mr. H*, he thought to himself. Charlene seemed to be getting a bit lax in their communication. Slowly, he replied to the message, making sure that his phrasing was very deliberate:

8:52 AM: *Charlene, I will be at the meeting. Please have my coffee ready upon my arrival and make sure that you are positioned the way that I like – Mr. Hartwood*

Knowing that his "Mr. Hartwood" salutation would make her nervous, he walked into his bedroom and prepared to get dressed. Wearing only the best clothes, today Donovan chose to adorn himself in his favorite blue button down shirt and a pair of nondescript black pants. Similar to most other material goods in his life, his clothes were custom fit and accentuated his muscles perfectly. As he looked into the mirror, Donovan fixed the buttons on his shirt so that the two at the top were left open. As he put on one of his many Rolex watches, Donovan couldn't believe the time. It was 9:15 and he was at least twenty minutes away from the office. As Donovan rushed out his bedroom door knowing that he'd have to skip breakfast, he briefly gave himself one last look in the mirror. With that, he took the elevator from his suite to the ground level of his spacious home and got into the limousine that was waiting for him. His chauffeur was new to his facility, a petite and pretty woman named Patrice. He actually had not personally hired her, but was told by his hiring manager that she would fit in nicely at the estate. From the looks of it, he could tell that she would. Patrice held the door open for him as he climbed inside his vehicle.

"You look great today Mr. Hartwood." Patrice said bashfully as she held the door open for her boss. It was obvious that she was nervous.

"You don't look so bad yourself, Patrice. That particular top really shows off your cleavage nicely." Donovan almost spat the words at his driver. He didn't like when women spoke out of turn, much less when they complimented him before he had a chance to offer them one first. Even though he was late, Donovan took a minute to stand over Patrice, making sure to take his time to look deliberately at her chest. Her black blouse was tight against her bosom, causing her breasts to nonchalantly bubble over the fabric that was preventing her rather large breasts from being revealed to him. Standing there, staring at her greedily and with little regard for her feelings, Donovan knew that he would not have to do much to get this tart to sleep with him. Today, unfortunately for her, he was running late. They would have to better acquaint themselves another time. Donovan gave her chest one more approving glance and then climbed into the back seat. Once Patrice was positioned back in the driver's seat, her eyes met with Donovan's through the rearview mirror. Donovan did not approve of this at all.

"Patrice, be a dear and position the front mirror so that I have full view of your lovely chest, if you don't mind."

"My...My pleasure Mr. Hartwood." Patrice moved the mirror so that their eyes could no longer meet. Instead, she turned the mirror down so that her mountainous breasts were in his full view. Still not satisfied with his control over her, Donovan addressed her again.

"Patrice...pull down your shirt a bit, I'd like to see more of your generous assets. Also, from now on you are refer to me only as Sir, not as Mr. Hartwood and certainly not as Donovan, until I tell you otherwise. Am I making myself clear?" As he toyed with her, Donovan could tell that he was eagerly waiting to see whether or not Patrice would follow his instructions. A new employee always had to be quickly broken in.

"Sir...if I pull my shirt down more I think that you'll be able to see...my nipples, Sir." Patrice sounded hesitant, as if she was considering refusing his order. Her voice was squeaky, and Donovan wondered if it might crack from the pressure that he was putting on her. His last driver often took off her shirt once Donovan had prompted her enough times to do so. Patrice would be no different, he was sure.

"Well it's a good thing that the windows are tinted, isn't it Patrice? What am I paying you for anyway, if I can't have a bit of fun on my way to work?" At first, she did nothing, but slowly Patrice used both of her hands to pull the front of her blouse lower, slightly revealing the outer edges of her areolas. Satisfied that she'd obeyed him enough for the time being, Donovan didn't want her to know that he was happy with her compliance. He barked at her, "Do you want me to be late for my meeting young lady? Let's get moving!" Startled, Patrice sat up straight in her seat and put in the car into drive. Donovan, Patrice, and her gratuitous breasts all took off towards the office.

Upon reaching the office, Patrice put the car in

park and immediately tried to fix her blouse. "What are you doing? Did I tell you to pull your shirt up?" Donovan knew that she didn't want to be seen like that in public, but he didn't care. If she was going to work for him, she would have to learn how to be less shy and more revealing. Surprisingly, Patrice did not seem too phased. Instead, she briskly got out of the limousine and walked around the car to the back-passenger door to let Donovan out. This time, she said nothing. Donovan made sure to stand over her the same way that he had when he first got into the car. His height compared to hers was considerable, and while her six-inch heels helped to accommodate this height difference, if an onlooker were to observe their interaction it would be obvious that Donovan's eyes were intently gaping at Patrice's chest. By this time in the morning, many of his employees, both men and women, were milling around the limousine and walking into the office. Little did Patrice know that while she felt embarrassed and heavily aroused by this encounter, many of Donovan's employees had seen him act in this manner before. After Donovan stared Patrice down for that seemed like an hour to her, he slowly brought his hands to her blouse and pulled it up himself so that her tits were securely back in her shirt.

"Pick me up at 4:30, sharp. On second thought, go to the receptionist and get my phone number. Text me so that I have your phone number, and if I need you to come get me earlier I will be in touch." With these words ending their brief encounter, Donovan looked her over objectively once more before turning his attention towards his massive office building. While heads were turning towards him and away from him because of the way in which he had just treated Patrice, Donovan hardly noticed. He was used to people staring at him, and in his mind, they were staring simply because he looked rugged and handsome, not because he had just sexually violated a woman publicly. He was certain that all of his employees enjoyed working for him too much to say anything anyway. His employees enjoyed their time working for Donovan because he had special rules and regulations in his office, many of which were unofficial and secretive in nature.

For example, anyone who worked for Donovan could take a two-hour lunch break each day. While this was a nice perk, there were stipulations to this leisure activity. No one could leave the premises during their lunch break unless it was approved ahead of time. An employee could instead spend his or her time in the nap room, the game room, the cafeteria, the tennis court, or take their time walking or running along the many trails that intercepted the office campus. While there were many nap rooms throughout the entire office building, it was a well-known secret to many that some nap rooms had secret doors within them. The cots that allowed for naps to be had could be moved to reveal doors that led to dimly lit hallways and winding staircases. If one were to move into these rooms, more beds would be revealed, but they would not the cots to hold single people. Instead, these beds were more spacious, allowing room for two or three people to "nap" at the same time. These rooms also housed lingerie, corsets, and sex toys that could be used by the employees at their leisure. Not only did Donovan frequently use these quarters to advance his own sexual preferences, but he also hoped that this type of employee-to-employee interaction would help to facilitate employee bonding and a sense of company togetherness. Additionally, a value that Donovan held dearly was the idea that sex should be casual amongst people. It was more fun that way, more carefree. He wanted to give his employees the same opportunity to live and work in an untroubled manner. If Donovan noticed that a particular couple or group of people were becoming too serious, he would talk to them and ban them from entering these quarters together. You see, he wanted the workplace to be lighthearted, not be grounds for relationship-making. In this way, he sought to control the sexual activity that went on in the office.

As Donovan opened up the doors to Hartwood Industries on this particular day, he was immediately greeted by a plethora of people. Regardless of his domineering nature or the fact that he sometimes acted inappropriately towards women, Donovan was the largest owner of the company. Because he was in such a notorious position, people easily forgot that he could act in perverse ways. Similar to his maids and butlers, both his male and female employees were compensated greatly for the time that they spent working at Hartwood Industries. Of course, while Donovan could rationalize having a female-only staff on his personal property (their jobs were largely thoughtless), he needed to be amongst men at the workplace. While he required no dress code for his male or female employees, he would sometimes send out email reminders to his female staff about the importance of looking professional and attractive simultaneously. It would sicken him to see his female employees come into the office looking ragged or unkempt. If Donovan noticed that the same employee was coming in looking shaggy or unprofessional, he would surely find a way to fire her. Of course, he kept this information mostly to himself.

CHAPTER 4

MISCONDUCT

As Donovan entered the elevator to take him to the highest level of the office, he began to get excited about his encounter with his secretary, Charlene. Charlene had proven over the years that she knew how to please him. Charlene was innocent in the sense that she knew how Donovan wanted to be treated, and she would go to great lengths to see that he was fully satisfied. Never once did he have to remind her to dress attractively while at the office, and this is one of the main reasons why she had become his right-hand lady. While only at an average height of five feet, five inches tall, Charlene's lightly toasted brown skin and almond colored eyes could coax any man into awe. Her demeanor had a gentleness to it that Donovan appreciated (although he would never admit it). It certainly helped Charlene professionally that in addition to her perfect skin and big eyes that her brown hair was wavy like a surfer's and was always placed in a manicured and deliberate way. Although she seemed gentle to her employer, Charlene was known to be aggressive when it was necessary. She was a professional at heart. She had been known to yell at people on the phone for trying to disturb Donovan while he was in important meetings, and she had told off many unrelenting women for Donovan in the past. She understood Donovan's nature, and yet was still susceptible to it. She would sometimes find herself wondering what it would be like to taste Donovan in her mouth and feel his body against hers. She had always wondered why Donovan had never pursued or demanded her in the way that he had other women. But she enjoyed her job and was slightly afraid of crossing boundaries that Donovan wanted to keep in place. She didn't want to get fired as so many other women had in the past.

That's not to say that Donovan didn't find Charlene attractive, but Donovan found that he often resisted demanding that Charlene wear skimpy outfits or go braless on casual Friday like he had for many other women who worked for him. It was hard for him to not notice that Charlene's personality was both snarky yet charming; however, Donovan did not naturally seem drawn to women like Charlene. Charlene could be commanding. She had a real presence. Often, Donovan seemed to prefer to watch her from afar rather than engage with her in an overly sexual way. Of course, she would still adhere to some of the guidelines that he had for her. Unlike other women that he sometimes encountered, she didn't seem to mind being used like a sex doll on display. It was part of their act. What was different about her was that he knew where her limitations seemed to start and end. It's safe to say that Charlene and Donovan's relationship was the closest thing that Donovan had to a friendship, yet even this friendship had sexual overtones that facilitated Donovan's bossy nature.

Lately however, it seemed as though Charlene had been toying with Donovan more than usual. As the elevator reached his office level, Donovan recalled the text that he had received from her earlier in the morning. That text was the first time that she had called him Mr. H. She usually referred to him exclusively as Sir or Mr. Hartwood. He figured that she would have to be reminded of her manners soon enough, just as all of the other women in his life had to be at one time or another. He also recalled the text that he had responded to her with: *Please have my coffee ready upon my arrival and make sure that you are positioned the way that I like.* As Donovan approached the large doors to his spacious and bright office, he could see his coffee waiting on his desk. He liked his coffee mixed simply. No sugar with just a touch of crème. That much remained the same. Positioned so that she was facing away from him bent over, he could see Charlene's plump behind nicely outfitted in black dress pants. While this was the way that he wanted her to be positioned, something seemed different today. Staring at her rump unabashedly, it took him a considerable about of time before he realized what was off. She had always been a good sport, playing along and acting like she didn't notice his stare, but today he realized that her G-string was fully exposed. Bent over and truly unaware of his presence, Donovan realized for a split second that it made him angry to see her exposing herself in this manner. She had never before shown her undergarments at the office. This was certainly a first.

This type of showmanship from Charlene seemed odd to him. Never before had she gone a step further than his basic command. For example, she would go braless at work sometimes, but would always make sure that her nipples were not fully exposed. She would wear low cut blouses, but would often slyly slink away from Donovan whenever he would get close to suggesting that she should show him more than what she was currently offering. If Charlene were being honest, she'd have to admit that most of the time her outfits were a byproduct of trying to fit in with the overall company culture at Hartwood Enterprises.

"Charlene, this is quite a surprise." Donovan tried to seem nonchalant, although he could feel small ripples of anger and uncertainty bubbling through his veins. He wasn't sure why. Charlene, seemingly undistracted by Donovan's arrival to the office, continued shuffling her papers with her bottom inches from his hand. It appeared that she really was looking for something important.

"Mr. Hartwood, sir, you told me to be in this position upon your arrival." Charlene's tone seemed distant, as if she were barely paying attention to Donovan's presence. This angered him even more. She continued, "It actually worked out perfectly, because the shareholders need the file on the merger plan with Google. They seem concerned about the future of the deal. I thought you should know, since you have to meet with them in a few minutes." Charlene continued rummaging through the contents of the filing bin. Without thinking, Donovan's fingers trailed to her exposed panties. Thinking about his experience with Nina earlier in the morning, Donovan became overcome with compulsion. Almost without thinking, he roughly grabbed the exposed part of Charlene's thong and pulled it back. It made a loud *snap* against her skin, causing her to jump to stand.

"Mr. Hartwood! Sir! Excuse me, but *how dare* you pull on my clothing like that!" Charlene felt exposed and betrayed. She had been under the impression that her interaction with Donovan was different from his interaction with other women. Of course, she agreed to prance around the office like a doll because she felt like that's what he wanted her to do, but they had their limits in how far they would go with one another. His actions were not normal to their typical correspondence.

"Charlene. I told you to get into your normal

position that I like to see you in everyday upon entering the office. You are to bend over and partake in filing from eight o'clock until ten o'clock each morning unless I say otherwise. Where in these instructions does it say to expose your panties? Your actions are basically asking me to touch your visible undergarments, and this is simply not acceptable for someone who is supposed to be following my exact orders. How else am I react upon seeing you like this?" Donovan's anger seemed palpable. It scared Charlene a bit to see him this way, but she was stubborn and not one to easily concede. She continued to confront him.

"Mr. Hartwood, I did not realize that my panties were exposed like this. If I had noticed, I surely would have hidden them from your view. I only try to do as I'm told in this office. I am the first to follow your orders to their exact specifications, but I'm afraid this type of harassment takes it too far. Do not touch me like that again." With those icy words, Charlene began to pick up the folder that she had dropped upon being groped by Donovan. She turned to walk away from him. He grabbed her arm.

"Charlene...I..." Donovan hesitated, not exactly knowing how to react to her defiant words. He felt slightly deflated. Women did not often respond to his seductive advances in this way. If he were being honest with himself, he didn't truly know why he had reacted to Charlene's exposure like this. He had looked at her legs and curvy attributes for years with little to no second thought. Yet here he was looking foolish to a woman who was supposed to know him better than most. Finally, Donovan found his words. "If you ever expose yourself in my office without my permission again, I'll fire you and blacklist you from every other employer in the Silicon Valley. Pull your pants up for Christ sakes.

Your unprofessionalism disgusts me." Donovan angrily turned away from Charlene and headed for the conference room. He was already running late and arguing with a low-level office staff member wouldn't make him any prompter. Charlene watched him walk away, angrily pulling up her pants and also heading for the conference room to hand over the Google folders that she had found.

CHAPTER 5

THOUGHTS CREEP IN

"Donovan, thank you gracing us with your presence. Do we have your permission to start the meeting now?" Everyone stood as Donovan entered the room, recognizing and giving due respect to the heir to the Hartwood name. Charlene trailed into the conference room behind Donovan, dropped off the merger files, and graciously excused herself from the meeting. Donovan sat down, fully engaged, as if totally forgetting about his abrupt interaction with Charlene only moments before. While not many women in his life treated him with much resistance when he made his advancements, he wasn't really surprised at Charlene. She required a tad too much respect for his taste anyway. *Although, I sure would have enjoyed seeing where the rest of those panties went*, Donovan mused.

"Okay," The boring inconspicuous office voice continued, "The next order of business is the prospective merger with Google. From the folders that Charlene dropped off, it looks like this might not pan out after all. We are suffering huge profit losses through the negotiations, and it looks like these losses are only going to get larger overtime." Donovan snapped back to full attention. Their merger with Google was supposed to bring even more money to his family's estate, and the deal was supposed to solidify his position as a real and legitimate negotiator within the company. If this deal fell through, Hartwood Enterprises could potentially lose millions of dollars in negotiation and patent fees. For these reasons, it was important to Donovan that this deal did not fail.

"What can we do to save the merger?" Donovan asked, suddenly completely focused on the task at hand. "Have we talked to our associates there? Maybe there's a chance they can strike some sort of understanding by working our contacts that already exist within the organization."

"Quite honestly, Donovan, it's not looking good. In order to save this thing, not only do we have to negotiate with Google, but we also have to rework our numbers to better reflect a sound profit from this whole thing. As it stands, Google would own a majority of the merger and we would be more like subsidiary partners." *Subsidiary partners.* Hearing those words together made Donovan's bones spasm.

Hartwood Enterprises was not about to become secondary, not even to the world's largest online conglomerate.

"This cannot happen. We either need to find a way to get ourselves a larger percentage of the profit, or we need to walk away." Donovan felt hollow, as if he soul depended on whether or not this merger happened.

"What we can do is call our contacts at Google and see if they can make something happen. At this point, that's our only option. If we can't convince Google to give us a larger share, all bets are off." A fellow shareholder spoke to Donovan matter-of-factly.

"Contact Google today and solidify the merger. Let me know as soon as you have a firm decision." With this, Donovan got up from his chair, causing the rest of the board members to rise as well. The news about the merger angered him, mostly because he had little control over the matter. While Hartwood Industries was a global enterprise, it paled in comparison to Google's worldly breadth and extensiveness. With little control over the situation in its entirety, Donovan huffed into his office and headed over to his mini bar. He poured himself a neat glass of Johnny Walker Black and he waited to hear from his associates about the deal.

One hour turned into two, and then three. Donovan got some more work done, talked to some of his co-workers, and grabbed a bite to eat in the cafeteria. While in the beginning of his tenure at Hartwood Industries, Donovan would often participate in most business deals personally, these days he had the money to pay qualified people to do this job for him. While he enjoyed the freedom that this luxury afforded him, he found that he could easily become bored or anxious because of this choice. After what seemed like half the day, his phone finally rang as he was headed back into his office after lunch. Slightly out of range to pick it up, Donovan's anxiety caused him to sort of prance towards the phone to ensure that he didn't miss the important phone call. It was one of his shareholders.

"It's not good, Don" the man's rugged voice spoke definitively in Donovan's ear. "Google has decided to move forward with their own technology. They have decided to decline our offer." Donovan produced silence into the phone as he swallowed the rest of his warm whiskey and it slid down his throat. He could feel it burning his belly, and for a moment he let this feeling consume him. Finally, he spoke. "Thank you for the call." He hung up just as quickly as he had answered the phone and began to pace around his office angrily. He didn't know what he was going to do. This potential merger had been one of the biggest deals that Hartwood Enterprises had in its future. Now that the deal had been a bust, he was going to have to work hard to find a new way to get its technology into the hands of another top technology company.

Donovan looked at the clock. It read 2:00 PM. He wasn't supposed to go home until around 4:00 PM, but the sour deal with Google had angered him to the point that he didn't really want to be in the office anymore. He busied himself with making one more drink, and then two. He knew that drinking usually caused him to be more aggressive generally, and he secretly didn't mind knowing that his aggression would be palpable upon his arrival home. As he sipped his whiskey, Donovan tried to turn his attention away from business and towards what awaited him later in the evening. As he thought about her schoolgirl outfit and other preparations that he was sure she was making by now, he couldn't help but indulge in the slightly degrading thoughts that were creeping into his head.

While he thought that the drinks would help ease his mind, they were actually causing him to think irrationally. Donovan often put on a good billionaire's face. It was hard to tell that he could have moments of unease and self-doubt. These types of thoughts usually had to do with the sometimes-harsh way that Walter regarded Donovan back when he was younger.

You can't even close a deal anymore. How are you going to maintain your wealth? You don't have kids now, but how are you going to continue a healthy legacy for your future children if you can't even secure funds for yourself now?

Your father is the only reason that you're wealthy. You've always been a mooch. What have you done for yourself besides sleep with a bunch of bimbos? They care about you as much as you care about them. You'll never find love, especially if you can't prove that you're successful.

Donovan found that these types of thoughts were hard to shake. After downing his fourth whiskey neat, he decided that it was time to call it a day. Looking at the clock, it was only 2:45 PM. *She's not going to be expecting me this early. That's probably for the best,* Donovan thought to himself. *This way, I can reprimand her for being unprepared.* Donovan got out his phone to text Patrice. Patrice had been a good girl and had texted Donovan her phone number so that they could be in contact throughout the day if Donovan needed a ride home early. *She's quickly learning to listen to my stern instructions*, Donovan pleasantly thought to himself. His mind was able to somewhat relax knowing that even if he couldn't control all of the business endeavors that he embarked upon at Hartwood Industries, he could at least control most women in his life to do as he said exactly as he intended. Except for Charlene. Donovan briefly thought back to the awkward encounter that he had with Charlene earlier in the day. In his tipsy stupor, he thought to himself, *she'll learn too.* He then downed the rest of his whiskey, buttoned up his shirt and fluffed his hair. He didn't want her to know that he had been drinking heavily. Donovan then pulled out his phone and texted Patrice.

3:04 PM: *I'm ready to be picked up, Patrice.*

3:04 PM: *Yes Mr. Hartwood, Sir. I'll be outside in two minutes, Sir.*

Donovan chuckled to himself internally. He was good at sensing weakness, and even through text he could tell that Patrice was nervous to see him again. He wondered if her breasts would be positioned as he had wanted them, or if he would have to teach her how to look whenever she picked him up. As he descended to ground level, he could see from afar that Patrice was standing by the open door of his limousine looking slightly flustered yet trying to appear confident. Her breasts were fully visible, the tops of her areolas in full view as the weight of her large breasts tried to topple the front of her blouse. Her legs looked magnificent in her skirt in the California sun, and Donovan paused as he watched his male employees gawk at her with primal sexual interest. Donovan allowed his cock to briefly twitch as he thought about bending Patrice over the hood of the limousine in broad daylight. He thought about the embarrassed excitement that she would feel if he were to demand her to get out of the limousine and spread her long legs apart. He pictured himself going up behind her and pulling up her skirt to reveal what was sure to be a firm and big rump. He would slowly raise the skirt, as if exposing a secret. He would even invite his other male employees to come take a closer look at her ample body. She would beg him to stop, but he wouldn't until her pleas turned into desire for him to ravage her to orgasm.

Shaking himself out of his fantasy, Donovan waited until his large and full cock became fully soft once more. He didn't want her to know what he had in store for her. Coming back to reality, Donovan walked quickly to his limousine where Patrice waited.

"Patrice, thank you for your promptness. I see that you have come to understand how I expect you to look each time you pick me up to take me to and from work?" Donovan made it a point to stand over her as he had when she had first opened the door for him. He could feel Patrice's eyes averting the darting stare that he was giving her, but this did not cause him to relent. Finally, Patrice's eyes met his, and he could see her apprehension and fear.

"Yes Mr. Hartwood, Sir. I fully understand how you expect me to look each day. Thank you, Sir." Donovan knew how badly Patrice was hoping that he would just get into the limousine, but he wanted to see how far he could push her."

"You know, Patrice, you seem to be a quick learner. I usually introduce my new employees to a few rules at a time, but it seems to me like you're ready for a few more." Donovan reached under her skirt and squeezed her flesh. He could feel the curve where her leg became her bottom, and he immediately approved. Patrice's rump was just as generous as her bosom. Slowly, he released her flesh from his grip and moved to feel her underwear. "I hope you understand, I need to make sure that you're following the dress code, down to every item of clothing. I see that you are in full compliance." Patrice's breath was growing heavy, he found that she had trouble finding the right words with which to respond. Finally, she answered.

"Yes Sir...Of course, I will always be in full compliance for you." Her knees were beginning to bend slightly, as if she were yearning for Donovan's fingers to feel for something else, something wet. Donovan looked around, and could see that a small crowd was beginning to form around his limousine where he and Patrice stood. As he removed his hand from under Patrice's skirt, he could tell that she was beginning to also notice the crowd. She quickly recoiled from him and tried to distance herself from his reach. This gave Donovan an idea.

"Patrice, while it seems that you are in full compliance with the dress code, how am I supposed to be fully sure that you aren't wearing different underwear than what I demand? I need to see them. Please, be a dear and take them off. Hand them to me." Donovan outstretched his hand and waited.

Patrice looked around helplessly, frantically searching for someone in the crowd who could save her. She only saw hungry eyes looking back at her. With nowhere to turn, Patrice bent down and slowly removed her panties from her body. Almost tripping as she stepped over them, she finally stood up and handed them disgracefully to her boss. Adequately satisfied with the humiliation that he had caused her, Donovan quietly got into the back seat of the limousine. Silent as they traveled back to the Hartwood Estate, Donovan knew that he had gotten to her. This proved that she would do as he said.

As they pulled up to his palatial home, Patrice quickly got out of the car and opened the back door for her boss. Meeting her gaze and he got out of the car, Donovan handed her back her panties. "If you wear panties to work again, you'll be fired immediately. Do we have an understanding?"

"Yes, Sir, I'm sorry Sir." Giving her one more

look over, Donovan roughly turned from her and headed into his property. He wouldn't think about Patrice for the rest of the evening.

CHAPTER 6

DONOVAN'S COMPULSION

Watching Patrice remove her panties in front of a crowd had certainly aroused Donovan. His arousal only grew as he felt her embarrassment over the entire situation, and this helped to quell some of the negatively that had occurred during his work day. Donovan glanced at his phone and took notice of the time. It read 3:15 PM. *At least she knows how to drive quickly,* Donovan thought to himself as he headed to his golf course. It was about a ten-minute walk to the golf course, but Donovan was in no rush. With the whiskey still coursing through his veins, Donovan was able to turn his mind to thoughts of finally relieving himself of the tension that had been in his pants since he had given Nina the spanking that she deserved earlier in the day. Upon reaching the golf course, Donovan sought out his custom-built golf cart and drove towards the outer edge of the Hartwood property. As the house and the golf course became smaller and out of focus, Donovan drove closer towards a heavily wooded area. To the average eye, this looked like the end of the Hartwood Estate, but Donovan knew what pleasantries were in store for him. Stopping the golf cart outside of the woods, Donovan got out of the golf cart and began walking through the woods. *I should have changed into my sneakers*, Donovan thought to himself. He realized that Patrice had gotten him more excited than he had realized. After walking through the woods for roughly five minutes,

Donovan came to a small cottage.

The outside of the cottage looked run down and dilapidated. Donovan took his keys from his pockets and found the one for this unit. It turned without controversy. Stepping inside of the small cottage, it was clear that the outside of the property had been designed to be deliberately shabby. Conversely, the inside was elaborately decorated. The small one bedroom dormitory held a kitchen with stainless steel appliances and butcher block countertops. There was also a small sitting area, with an oriental rug and white leather sofa giving the space aesthetic comfort. As Donovan opened the door to the home, he did he best to keep quiet. He didn't want her to expect him.

Taking off his shoes, Donovan silently moved from the living room into the bedroom. While the entire unit was nice, the bedroom had clearly been built with the most care. The king-sized bed was sitting on top of a luxurious bed frame. It was hard to not notice the giant metal rings that hung from either side of the head board, perfect for tying a helpless woman to. Laying under the covers, her head barely exposed, was a blonde headed woman. Donovan could see the covers moving up and down where the woman was laying. He knew exactly what she was doing. She hadn't noticed him enter the room, and Donovan watched silently as her breath grew ragged and louder. Before her breathing became almost moan-like in quality, Donovan grabbed the covers and pulled them off of the woman. Startled, she looked around, clearly surprised that she had been caught.

The woman was wearing white lingerie. The thigh highs and stockings opened in the middle to reveal crotch-less panties. She was not wearing a top. Her breasts and clit, swollen from the pleasure that she was giving herself, looked full and engorged. Trying to pull the covers back over her, the woman quickly shoved what she was holding under her body in an attempt to keep it out of Donovan's view.

"Mr. Hartwood, I wasn't expecting you for at least a half hour. Why didn't you ring me?" The woman's thick accent permeated the room and mixed with the sweet smell of sex that was emanating from her lustful body.

"Who are you to question me, Veronica? Stand up." Donovan ordered Veronica to rise, knowing that she would have to reveal her toy to him. She hesitated, and tried to talk her way out of the situation in which she found herself.

"Sir, please, you must understand. I was trying to wait for you to come over, but I was feel so aroused I could barely contain myself. I was thinking about last time and it was driving me wild."

"You know that I expect you to be freshly washed and sanitized when I come over. You're not even showered. I've had a long day at work and was expecting to see a schoolgirl ready to listen to my commands. Instead, I find a foolish girl pleasuring herself with a vibrator that I didn't even know she had. Hand it over." Donovan again outstretched his hand. Veronica crawled to his hand and bashfully placed a small pink vibrator into his hand. Donovan angrily put it into his pocket and grabbed the girl by the arms.

"You are disobedient. When will you learn to be more compliant? I don't ask much from you, only that you dress the way that I like and that you're ready for me when I come over." Shaking the girl, Donovan enjoyed watching her naked breasts bounce up and down. Roughly, Donovan flipped Veronica over so that she was laying on her belly. He spanked the girl at least ten times, watching with delight as her bottom reddened from the contact with his hand. With each *spank*, he yelled at her to make sure that she knew why she was being punished.

"Do you think I'm stupid, Veronica? Did you think I wouldn't notice your swollen lips?"

"No sir! I'm sorry, sir!" Veronica cried out, the agony from the contact with Donovan's hand was both painful and arousing.

Satisfied that she had received the proper number of spanks, Donovan grabbed his prisoner and dragged her face down towards the rings hanging from the head board. He grabbed the sheet from the bed and ripped it in half, then used these rags to tie her hands to either side. With her arms splayed, he then moved towards her legs. Spreading them wide, he roughly dipped a finger into her vagina. His finger was sopping wet when he removed it from the girl's swollen pussy. He reentered the girl, this time rubbing her clit, causing her to scream with delight. This behavior continued for twenty minutes. Her fluids began to pool on the bed, creating a puddle on the sheets.

"You're making a mess, Veronica. Maybe if you hadn't pleasured yourself before I got here, you wouldn't be leaking all over the place." He stopped fingering her and took out the vibrator from his pocket with her noticing. Turning it on, Veronica's body began to gyrate. She knew that this instrument was intended for her. She began to protest.

"Mr. Hartwood, please, if you put that inside of me I won't be able to contain myself. I'm going to have to orgasm." Veronica, face down, pleaded with Donovan to put away her toy, but he simply shoved her face into the pillow so that he could no longer hear what she was saying. Her moans grew louder as Donovan shoved the vibrator into her dripping vagina.

"You are not to reach orgasm until I say so, Veronica. You have already disobeyed me enough for one day." Knowing how hard this would be for her, Donovan did not continue to press the vibrator into her for very long. Stopping, she sighed, relieved for a moment to regroup. He pulled down his pants and then propped up her hips, making her vaginal lips fully visible. Setting himself up and without warning, Donovan plunged his erect cock into Veronica and began pumping her with all of the energy that he had pent up from the day. Veronica, screaming with delight, could wait no longer. He felt her vaginal muscles contracting against his thick pulsating cock. Her tightness proved too much for him to bear. He quickly exited her and shot his orgasm on her low back. Veronica's body collapsed on the bed, her arms still splayed out wide. She tried to turn so that she could face Donovan, but he got up to grab a cigarette and simply left her there, alone.

Donovan's ritual after spending time with Veronica was to have a smoke and a nap on the white leather couch in the living room. Sometimes, he would untie her and they would nap together, and other times he would leave her tied to the bed and sleep alone. Today, he would sleep without her. Lying down on the couch and bringing the cigarette to his lips, Donovan closed his eyes. He was tired from today's activity. Puffing out the smoke from his cigarette, Donovan began to drift off to sleep. As the thoughts from the day drifted away from him, an image came into his head. It was blurry at first, but as it came into focus, he realized that it was Charlene. *Why am I thinking about Charlene right now? I just had great sex with Veronica*, Donovan pondered over his brain's confusion. The first image that he had was Charlene bent over the filing cabinet with her thong prominently displayed, but as he drifting deeper into sleep, these images became less sexual and more normal. Charlene and him were sitting at a dining table. They were laughing together, her dimples coming into full view. In one last lucid attempt, Donovan tried to shrug his thoughts of Charlene from his head. He subconsciously knew that if these thoughts persisted, he would have to confront them in the only way that he knew how, *through controlling sex.* The problem was that he wasn't sure whether or not Charlene would be receptive to his dominant ways, rather it was her potential resistance that might entice his true nature.

Will Donovan pursue Charlene, the one woman who he knows will be the toughest one to seduce, or will he refuse the challenge and ignore his lustful thoughts? Find out in the next book of the

Billionaire's Series: Fascination.

www.ingramcontent.com/pod-product-compliance
Lightning Source LLC
LaVergne TN
LVHW010409070526
838199LV00065B/5922